BLACKBOARD BUNGLE

BY
LEONARD SCHWARTZ

PublishAmerica
Baltimore

First printing

ISBN: 1-4137-6721-4
PUBLISHED BY PUBLISHAMERICA, LLLP
www.publishamerica.com
Baltimore

Printed in the United States of America

TABLE OF CONTENTS

I. Unforgettable Characters and Events

II. Administrative Gaffes

III. Bureaucratic Bungling

IV The Final Chapter

FOREWORD

T eaching in an urban environment can be both rewarding and extremely stressful. I know. I've been there for over thirty years. It's the only profession I know where at times the client and the practitioner are adversaries. In some cases it seems like the patient is trying to stab the doctor during the operation.

The book was written not to impugn the industrious, dedicated teachers and administrators who make up more than 90% of the system, but to shed a comedic light on people and incidents one faces during an extended period of employment.

If people recognize themselves, it is purely coincidental or guilty feelings. The characters and anecdotes portrayed make up a compilation of people and events from several schools, which shall remain nameless and placeless.

The names of people and places have been changed.

The majority of hardworking and no-nonsense educators should not in any way feel maligned at this humorous attempt.

1

UNFORGETTABLE CHARACTERS AND EVENTS

YES, IT'S WITCHCRAFT

He had the voice and charisma of an established Hollywood actor. The students awaited his every word. Yet Mr. Denton was suspended several times from different schools before his termination in the 1980s.

Mr. Denton was an idealistic, gifted, young teacher who was going to change the establishment. However, in trying to achieve his goals, his personality underwent a transformation in the late sixties and early seventies.

He became totally involved in devil worship and Satanism. All his lessons revolved around the good-versus-evil theme with the occult always dominating the lesson. In all his teachings he was the good; the school administration, the evil. His stories were so hair raising that many students were petrified to enter his room, lest he put a spell on them. When he told the class that there would be a spelling test on Friday, they weren't quite sure what he meant.

Nevertheless, some students who were really into black magic and the occult even joined his secret lunchtime club. When the administration got wind of what was transpiring, he was told to cease and desist immediately, to no avail. His supervisor, Mrs. Fremer, observed a lesson and declared him

9

incompetent in front of the class. Denton retorted that she was incompetent with the students roaring at every word. Mrs. F. related what occurred to the principal and Denton was mandated to drop devil worship from his curriculum.

This did not deter him. He proceeded to hang the principal in effigy inside his classroom and burned him in front of the class. He also told them countless stories of his membership in Hell's Angels, a Greenwich Village motorcycle gang of that era.

When parental complaints reached the school, Denton began wearing a full satanic costume. We would often see him in devil's garb chasing students down the hall, pitchfork in hand. He even accused and threatened traveling teachers, who occasionally used and "destroyed" his room, that they would be cursed for life.

He was so paranoid that he believed that the FBI was tailing him. He often told passengers in his vehicle that he had to take special routes to lose the Feds who were following him.

One day he came to work pajama clad claiming his mother evicted him in the middle of the night. When he pointed a toy gun at the principal's secretary, it was the straw that broke the camel's back.

Denton was suspended and ordered to undergo psychiatric rehabilitation. He resurfaced a few years later in a high school dressed as a Nazi storm trooper. After a second stint at rehab, he eventually latched on to another high school position, where he propositioned many female students, telling them bizarre stories of how he would get them jobs to pose for girlie magazines.

Finally, we read that Denton was one of five teachers terminated by the Board of Education for improper conduct. If you knew how difficult that procedure is, you could appreciate the scope of his behavior.

MERCURY MAN

Mercury Man was a science teacher who had a penchant for frequenting the ladies' lavatory. Since his room was only steps away from the women's bathroom, he felt that it was an imposition and waste of time for him to walk up and down the stairs to the men's room. He related this message to female employees on countless occasions.

Why is he called Mercury Man? One day, while conducting an experiment, Mr. Mercury had the entire class touch samples of mercury. His room was quarantined for several weeks while the poison control center sanitized it.

Furthermore, Mr. M. had a speech impediment. How can a pedagogue, who is supposed to impart knowledge in a clear and concise manner, be effective when students could only comprehend every fifth word? To his charges and some colleagues he was known as "Old Marble Mouth."

In order to cope and get through the day, it was rumored that Mercury possessed a bottle of liquor secured in a brown paper bag on the top shelf of his clothing closet. Mercury's speech impairment plunged him into many difficult situations. More about Mercury Man in "Lost in the City."

BIG BIRD

Mr. Maloney, a retired civil servant, embarked on a second career, teaching. The students dubbed him "Big Bird" because of his tremendous height and other physical features that resembled the famed cartoon character. His behavior also resembled an animated character right out of the comic strips or from Disneyland.

Maloney commenced his teaching career when most others were in or contemplating retirement. A hearty ha-ha or ho-ho would greet his students. However, there was one major problem with Mr. M. He would literally and figuratively talk to the wall. By that, I mean that very few students paid attention to him. Perhaps a select group of four or five would come up front to learn. The rest was strewn about the room talking, playing cards, or creating mayhem. Big bird seemed oblivious to it all.

One day, Bird was attempting to teach a "review" lesson for the midterm. While he was engaged with three students, four others, unbeknownst to him, opened a window and climbed outside. They then proceeded to walk gingerly along the edge of the building, five floors high. Eventually they passed the window of the assistant principal, who happened to be turning toward the window ensconced in his swivel chair. Not believing what he witnessed, he took a double take and immediately ran next door to usher the students back in via the window of the next room. A disaster had been prevented.

Mr. Siegel, the savior, then escorted the gang of four to BB's room. Big Bird welcomed them, never having any idea what just transpired.

Maloney was as notorious as an athlete. He attempted to keep up with the younger staff members on the basketball court, but his court antics were similar to his teaching ones. BB was so into sports that even while on hall patrol, he couldn't resist exhibiting his athletic prowess.

"Hey, kid, go out for a pass," he screamed while stationed near the AP's office. He tossed a football down the hall but missed his intended receiver. The ball traveled by an open door, where the class inside had a perfect view. This caused about one quarter of the class to vacate the room in order to retrieve the ball. In the confusion, the loose ball was kicked down the stairs to the fourth floor, chased by at least twenty students. By the time all was said and done, a mini-riot had occurred. Eighty students from various classes on two floors were after the elusive football.

Big Bird was on hall duty to ensure the safety of the students. What he had accomplished by becoming a quarterback was to create the very scene he was supposed to prevent. Eventually, the administration forced him to transfer to another school.

If you think his teaching was horrific, you should have seen him behind the wheel of an automobile. Whenever he was on the road, the probability of an accident increased by one thousand percent. He would complain that these young drivers had no respect for the old-timers. Wouldn't you let an elderly gentleman speed through red lights at sixty miles per hour on crowded city thoroughfares?

WALKMAN

If you ask people in today's society what a walkman is, they'll tell you about radios and earphones. If you ask a staff member in my school, you would probably hear about Mr. Sanders, the marathon walker.

Mr. Sanders walks for health; doctor's orders. The only time that you don't see him parading around the hall is when he is teaching. Then, he's usually firmly ensconced in his chair.

Nothing can prevent the Walkman from his daily routine of five miles. If you wish to converse with him, you must catch him on the "walk," or else no conversation. Occasionally, if he must refrain from walking, he'll speak to the principal or her assistant while jogging in place.

One June day, when the students were particularly rowdy, the principal ordered all deans and assistant principals into the hallway, chairs and desks included, for the balance of the week. Her opinion was that this maneuver would eliminate student traffic in the halls during class time. Have you ever seen administrators set up a makeshift office in the hall? It's quite interesting.

To further complicate matters, at that particular time, the assistants were in the midst of conducting interviews for next year's open teacher positions. Get the picture?

While all of this craziness was occurring—desks in the hall, AP's doing paperwork and conducting interviews, teachers standing in line around the desks—who should appear? The Walkman, attired in his typical garb of jeans, sneakers, and T-shirt, began jogging around a desk during an interview while students were passing during a change of periods. What a sight. It should have been videotaped.

Sanders seemed unphased at the criticism leveled at him and continued his habit until he decided to transfer to another school. Rumor had it that the new school had an indoor track.

Perhaps if you visit or are employed in his current school, you might view a person walking in the halls, book in hand, headphones around his head. If you do, then you'll know who he is.

Arms for the Poor

It's unusual for a husband and wife to teach in the same school for obvious reasons. Some sources say it's illegal. Nevertheless, Mr. and Mrs. Hooper managed it.

Mrs. Hooper was extremely quiet, almost secretive. You may have never known she existed until you discovered that she took a nasty spill and was injured in the line of duty. After the fall, winter, and spring, she was never seen or heard from again.

Mr. Hooper, on the other hand, was the more recognizable and outspoken member of the duo. He would often give dissertations about how important the curriculum was and how he slavishly worked to get the point across to his students. Yet when you noticed him snoozing at his desk or trying to control a disruptive class by leaving them alone, you might think he was not being totally honest with you.

Hooper seemed a bit strange to many people. He began his service as a substitute teacher. Whenever a teacher was absent he would take over the class and its contents for the day. His penchant for paperwork was so thorough that many teachers were unable to locate their teacher editions and other important documents upon their return, even though these items were buried deep in a locked desk drawer or a secure closet. What they didn't realize was that Hooper possessed a unique key ring. It appeared to contain approximately three hundred keys, some of which were master keys. How he obtained them remained a mystery.

One day I tested my theory about the master keys. I inadvertently locked my school keys inside my clothing closet. I had no alternative but to call the custodian to break the lock. What else could I do? I decided to call Mr. Hooper. He took a quick look and immediately opened my personal lock with one of his keys.

Later that week, my wife and I donated clothing at a Goodwill box in a nearby shopping center. As we placed the bag inside the bin, we seemed to hear a voice inside, but discounted it. About a week later, to my surprise, I saw Mr. Hooper wearing one of the shirts I just had disposed of. How, may you ask, did I know for sure that it had been mine? First of all, the color and design were unique. It was a pink shirt with maroon flowers. The real proof was the ink marks on the sleeve and the unmistakable brown stain located on the upper left shoulder.

When my wife and I discussed what occurred, we then thought about the voice we heard inside the bin. Perhaps there was someone inside. What if that someone was waiting with "open arms" for a gift of clothing? What if it were Hooper?

STINKY SHMOTTA

Mr. Felix, a gentleman in his sixties, was an unforgettable character. He would stack every drawer, cabinet, and even refrigerator in the teachers' room with rexographed worksheets. If you saw the movie *Teachers*, he's the mirror image of "Ditto" or vice versa. Nobody was able to store any materials or food supplies in the TR because of this.

Felix was also an exceptional dresser. Not that I'm a fashion plate, but it seemed as though he wore the same clothing day after day. Perhaps he even slept in them. It had that wrinkled or prewrinkled look. The garb consisted of a creased shirt, suspenders, cuffed pants hanging to the floor, and scuffed shoes. A faculty member dubbed him "Stinky Shmotta," which translates to smelly rags.

One day Stinky strolled into the teachers' room at lunchtime. To my surprise, after inventorying his worksheets, he sat down and began to eat. What was so incredible about the sandwich he was digesting was that one half came from his cuff and the other half was pulled from his shirt pocket. I noticed that he actually had a slice of buttered bread lodged in his left cuff, perhaps a snack for later. To complete the sandwich, he extracted a piece of chicken out of his left pocket and another slice of bread from his left shirt pocket. All items were neatly unwrapped. This was called the "SM" special.

Later that year we learned that his wife was in the building looking for him. Not wanting to miss the sight of these mates together, half the faculty stormed downstairs. We were shocked.

In the main office stood a beautiful woman, immaculately and stylishly attired. Though getting on in years, she appeared ten to fifteen years younger than Stinky. We looked at each other wondering how this could be. She and SM? Was she really his spouse?

Perhaps he gave all of himself to her, or maybe he was hiding his real persona. In all likelihood, opposites attract, in more ways than one would suspect.

SEE HOW
THEY RUN

Mr. Romano was a likeable and courageous teacher. The fact that he was blind added to his woes. For some strange reason, many students took advantage of his disability instead of sympathizing with him. Even though he had a full-time assistant in the classroom, Mr. Romano encountered numerous problems.

Instead of trying to assist him, the administration attempted to oust him for incompetence. The principal tried to intimidate him by requesting that he leave his position in order to receive a satisfactory rating. If not, then he'd be rated unsatisfactory, which could have led to Romano's termination.

Mr. R. fought this blind man's bluff all the way to the civil court and emerged victorious. The school administrators were berated for insensitivity and using discriminatory practices against the handicapped.

However, Romano still had a difficult time. In spite of the court's ruling, a second principal tried similar tactics. Romano was even assigned hall patrols (the blind leading the blind?). Mr. Romano remained steadfast, fought again and won.

Several years later, another enlightened principal tried to force him out by offering a traveling program, not in his license area, without an aide. Mr. R. filed a union grievance, which stopped this current round of administrative misbehavior.

Finally, Romano retired on his own terms. He is enjoying his retirement and is a prominent member of the Guild for the Blind.

What happened to the three principals (stooges) who tried to terminate him? They should be taking courses in human relations and collecting funds for the Guilt for the Blind. They can be seen running into the sunset, chased by a courageous, blind man. See how they run!

TICKET TO NOWHERE

Mr. Santiago seemed to be just what the doctor ordered. He was well educated and appeared to be sincerely interested in the education of his students. He was a role model for many children.

Santiago was extremely quiet, almost shy, but had the aggressiveness to turn many students around. As a probationary teacher, he was learning his craft while working, not unlike many others in the system.

Things went smoothly for him until late one spring. Santiago had organized a trip to Great Adventure, an amusement park in New Jersey. For what seemed to be a reasonable fee, students and their parents were to receive a bus trip, admission, and unlimited rides at the famed recreation park.

On the Saturday morning they were scheduled to go, the participants arrived bright and early with hopes of a great day flashing in their minds. You could see the joy in their faces as their banter became louder. However, their smiles eventually turned to frowns as time went on. Where was Mr. Santiago? Where were the buses? Weren't they supposed to leave at 8 a.m.? It was almost eight and nobody was there except them. Eight o' clock turned to nine and everyone dejectedly left, shaking their heads in disbelief. What went wrong? Since they could not contact Mr. Santiago on the weekend, they had to wait until Monday for an explanation.

On Monday Mr. Santiago politely explained to their astonishment that they had the date wrong. The trip was scheduled for the following Saturday. Most were satisfied, but a few skeptical and irate parents demanded a refund and investigation. Naturally, all the funds were in the hands of the tour operator, according to Mr. S. The principal took a wait and see attitude.

When next Saturday rolled around, the same thing happened. Now they were all ready to revolt. After the screaming and yelling ceased on Monday morning, Santiago calmly explained that the bus had mechanical problems. When asked why he wasn't at the school to notify them, he responded by stating that he, too, was on the bus and there was no means of contacting the school. He assured everyone that next Saturday there would be no problem.

Do I have to tell you what didn't transpire next Saturday? Mr. S. failed to show again. But this time, he failed to show up for work as well. Efforts were made to contact him, to no avail. He had disappeared and so did everyone's money.

Mr. Santiago never returned. Rumors circulated that he had a gambling and/or drug problem. The trip he organized was actually a trip to nowhere in more ways than one. For he, too, seemed to be headed in the same direction.

PARA-NOID OR PARA(N)NOYED?

In his heyday, Mr. Marcus was an excellent social studies teacher. In the late 1950s, when I was a student at a nearby junior high school, he was considered a master teacher. The first day we entered his class, his remark of nobody gets higher than an 85 brought tears to the eyes of half the class.

Mr. Marcus had a lot of insight into education. At that time, he taught and focused in on reading as a subject. For the life of me, I couldn't understand why. Yet, a decade later, I became a reading teacher thanks to Mr. Marcus, my mentor. This position has lasted for over thirty years. Mr. M. was truly a visionary.

When I arrived at the school, Marcus was the reading coordinator and part-time teacher. He was extremely helpful to new teachers, but was having problems in the classroom. The students of the 70s and 80s were far different from their predecessors.

Showing true professionalism, Marcus never complained while giving it his best in all areas. After all, didn't he survive the "down with the fat man" rallies and win the Elmer Fudd look-a-like contest when I was a student in his class?

As the students became even more difficult and the reading scores plummeted, Mr. Marcus, getting on in years, was under extreme pressure from the administration to "raise the reading scores." To add to his woes, he was in charge of the paraprofessionals (classroom teacher aides and assistants). Many of the paras were community residents, who were hired to assist reading and math instructors while attending college part time to pursue their own teaching degrees. The paras and Marcus did not see eye to eye much of the time. Many resented his demanding style and refused to cooperate with him. In turn, Mr. M. felt extremely uncomfortable around the paras because they often publicly humiliated him and threatened his authority. He became so obsessed and angry with his relationship with them that colleagues believed he was para-noid or para-(n)noyed.

Things went from bad to worse for my former teacher. The administration, tired of low reading scores and his poor relationship with the paraprofessionals, relegated him into the classroom on a full-time basis. After all, a scapegoat was needed for inferior student performance on standardized reading examinations.

Marcus saw the writing on the wall. Now in his sixties, he was not about to accept a demotion to a position of his youth. Reluctantly, he decided to retire.

That's what some administrators do. If they don't like you or your performance, or they desire to hire a politically connected person, they make life so uncomfortable and miserable that you'll transfer, resign, or retire. Yesterday's heroes are today's punching bags.

So it went with Mr. Marcus. Not long after his retirement, we sadly learned that my former teacher and mentor had passed away. A note over the time clock in the main office mentioned his untimely passing.

Not much of a fuss was made. School officials, for the most part, only care about what you can do for them tomorrow, not what you have already accomplished.

FROM WALL STREET TO SESAME STREET

In the 1950s, Mr. Baxter, a bespectacled stockbroker, became disillusioned with life on Wall Street. Wanting to contribute to society in a different way, he opted to become a teacher.

When I entered the profession, Baxter had already established himself as one of the premier teachers in the city. An avid reader and traveler, Mr. B. seemed to love his second profession. As the years passed, he became frustrated again. If you spoke to him at great length, you were surprised to discover that he was not a professor at some ritzy Ivy League college. His liberal tendencies overcame his desire to head for the elite campus life.

Mr. Baxter was quite a character. He had a marvelous sense of humor and was quite the practical joker. Furthermore, he had a dark side, which made him prone to fits and temper tantrums.

One day while walking through the corridor, I observed a bizarre situation in progress. Mr. Morrison, Baxter's social studies supervisor, was attempting to enter Mr. B's room, where my homeroom class happened to be that particular period. The only problem was that Baxter denied Morrison access. You had to be there! Two adult educators, on each side of the door, pushing and shoving that door like combatants in a wrestling match. Shouts of "Let me in!" and "You're not coming in!" were emanating from their angry vocal cords. Meanwhile, my official class was roaring. The two "role models" were exhibiting more immature behavior than the class in front of them would ever show. Mr. Morrison finally relented and walked away to the delight and cheers of the class.

Another time, Baxter's door flew open and a student book bag went soaring down the hall. A yell of "Get the hell out here" was followed by a student scurrying after the bag. Trying to force his way back into the room, student and teacher engaged in a shouting match highlighted by various threats of bodily harm.

Baxter loved to make fun at the idiosyncracies of the staff and administration. He was an independent thinker who refused to be bullied. When challenged by administrators' weird requests, he often told them where to go. To the principal he charged, "Are you a psychiatrist and mind reader? How do you know what I'm thinking?" His perverse sense of humor could be seen in skits at the end term parties, which usually turned into a roast of the current administration.

He often played tricks on his best friends too. Since he knew that a certain pedagogue often complained of a cold room, he'd arrive early in the winter and devilishly open her windows as wide as possible. This particular teacher, infamous for her complaining, moaning, and groaning about the most trivial item, was dubbed Princess Mona by Baxter.

Near the end of his career, Baxter was really fuming. He was disgusted with the "Nazi-like" tactics by certain administrators and vowed to get even. One morning, a "spy" for the administration reported that Mr. Baxter was blocking the entrance to his room by placing a filing cabinet near the door. He was told to move it immediately.

When Baxter vociferously refused, an assistant principal was sent to warn him. Mr. Baxter was adamant. He explained that due to structural damage in his room, the cabinet had to be placed by the door.

When the principal appeared and repeated the same message, it was just too much for Baxter to take. The two had harsh words and Mr. B's presence was requested in the principal's office at the beginning of the next period. Never one to be upstaged, Mr. Baxter beat him to the punch. He pulled out a previously completed application for retirement, signed on the dotted line, and handed it to the principal. He then calmly strolled out of the building never to be seen again.

PRINCESS MONA

What was that noise coming from the teachers' room? Was someone sick, injured, or dying? No. It was coming from a teacher who was lying across two sofas, preventing others from sitting. This was Princess Mona, aptly named by Mr. Baxter, for her constant whining and moaning.

Besides moaning, she was always whining and complaining about such mundane topics as family relationships, lost boyfriends, and the state of education. The worse the situation became, the louder she moaned. One day the princess caught her breast in the desk drawer, which caused moaning like we never heard before, and rightly so. The principal, attempting to keep abreast of the situation, scrutinously examined the injury and pronounced her fit to return to work immediately. However, she was in such pain that every step of the trek to the top floor caused moans louder than the previous ones.

Princess M. was also responsible for the artwork and illustrations in the school yearbook. One year, she drew all the administrators drowning in a sinking ship. They were under water, swimming for their lives, without a clue. Quite symbolic, wouldn't you say?

This incurred the wrath of one assistant principal who was so angry that she seemed to have daggers in her eyes. At the next meeting of the yearbook committee, she told staff members that when they see Mona, they should relay an unspeakable and unprintable message to her. At the time, the princess was sitting only a few seats away. The two did not speak to each other for several weeks.

If she weren't lamenting the lack of well-behaved students, she was crying about her parents' intrusiveness into her love life. She went on and on about how it was their fault that several potential husbands left her.

Eventually, she slipped on that infamous banana peel and tumbled down a flight of stairs. Disability sounded good because she could now remain at home and bemoan her unpleasant existence. Perhaps modeling for large women, now in vogue, would be her next career. So, with a disability pension secured, we now moan the loss of her employment.

LET'S DO IT THE FRENCH WAY

On the surface, Mr. Zabel appeared to be a dedicated French instructor who was rather strict. He was so into his profession that he once escorted several students to a French restaurant on his own time. However, as time went on, he experienced a personality metamorphosis becoming extremely combative and argumentative.

At first, it was evident in classroom exchanges between students and teacher when Zabel verbally embarrassed them. One Open School Night a heated exchange of words between an irate parent and Mr. Z. nearly led to fisticuffs. Playing the peacemaker, I stepped in and restored order.

His behavior then became even more bizarre. He often boasted that he was engaged in extramarital affairs with many women in his apartment complex. I'd call that a complex problem. I also witnessed his palm-reading escapade one summer at a local beach club. Reading from a book on palmistry, he informed my spouse that she had little time left based on her lifeline displayed in her palm.

Mr. Z. tried to divert his anger towards athletics and eventually become a marathon runner. In doing so, he lost so much weight that he barely weighed ninety pounds. Since his behavior did not improve, the administration finally got fed up. They requested that he transfer, but he adamantly refused. They changed his teaching program three times one September to induce him to leave. Still, he refused to go.

Then, one day, we noticed Mr. Zabel packing his belongings. "They've eliminated French and I'm out of here," he stated. His odyssey of school changes was underway.

At one school, he failed approximately 90% of the class. When the principal challenged him, he refused to alter any of the grades. He was brought up on charges of insubordination and approached the local media for assistance. For the next two weeks cameras, reporters, and microphones surrounded the school. He finally agreed to a non-teaching position at the district office.

After a few years Zabel rediscovered his religious roots and became a born-again zealot. This seemed to fit his personality perfectly. Zabel was always fanatical about any venture or discussion that he was involved in. He later returned to the school that exiled him, only to transfer a short time later. Due to bureaucratic red tape he was forced to return a third time. That was the last I heard of him.

While he taught at my school, Mr. Z. used to karate chop wooden bookends in front of the class to show his superior strength. The wood was composed of sandpaper.

Another weird incident occurred while he taught in room 511 at my school.

During the lesson, the ceiling caved in. Mr. Lewis, the assistant principal, immediately rushed to the site and successfully steered everyone out of harm's way. About fifteen years later, Mr. Zabel was again teaching in room 511 at a similarly constructed school.

The building was identical to the previous one in every way and this time, Mr. Lewis was his principal. The ceiling caved in with Mr. Lewis rushing to the rescue. These two incidents symbolized Mr. Zabel's teaching career.

THE RAZOR'S EDGE

Mr. Whitestone, a former staff developer at a nearby school, was curiously transferred to our school. It turned out that Mr. W., who had a history of drug abuse, was caught in the act on the job.

At first, the change of scenery combined with rehabilitation appeared to help.

He stayed out of trouble and taught his classes in an exemplary manner. However, as the term progressed, indicators such as lateness for work and class, absenteeism and weird tales of personal woe, combined with student confrontations negatively affected his behavior and performance.

By the spring, stories were circulating that he was back on drugs. He claimed that his former spouse as well as his current flame were giving him a hard time. Furthermore, he was in the process of being treated for a cancerous tumor, while on another front, his landlord had begun eviction proceedings. The signs were evident. Whitestone had taken a step backward in his rehab.

Then, a bizarre event occurred. In late June, while approaching his automobile in the school parking lot, he was attacked. Mr. W. was admitted to a local hospital with facial and neck cuts from the perpetrator's razor. Was it a random attack or drug related? No one knows for sure, but the rumor was that Whitestone had been involved in a drug deal that went sour. We never found out the truth.

Mr. Whitestone recovered and was quickly transferred to another school district.

Hopefully, he's on the road to a complete recovery.

BONDING

Mr. Charles was an enigma. He was a pleasant sort of fellow, but you'd never know the real Mr. Charles unless you read about him in the newspaper.

Charles was a member of the science department who was considered a loner.

Curiously, he used to grade students ninety percent on their report cards when they were truant. Perhaps he enjoyed not having them around. It was no great surprise that attendance in his classes was rather sparse. At times, he was the only one present, offering further proof of his loner status. Yet, he confided in me that he was unhappy working here and would prefer teaching in a school closer to his home.

Mr. Charles had a most unusual background. He formerly ran a gambling casino in Europe before moving to the states. That might explain what transpired later on.

One day, about a year after his transfer, we heard a news report that federal law enforcement officials had stopped a car on a New Jersey interstate highway. The driver had a handsome sum of stolen bearer bonds in his possession. Can you guess who the driver was?

Mr. Charles was arrested, but proclaimed his innocence. Everyone in the school was in a state of shock. How could a Clark Kent-type like Charles be involved with bond thieves?

Thinking back to his European gambling connection, it was not beyond the realm of possibility. No one really knows anyone, except if you live with them; and even then, there are people with dark sides, some of whom lead double lives.

We never read another line about the case or heard from Mr. Charles again. I hope that his principal rated him 90% when he was not in his classroom.

HE'S A
TRAVELING MAN

When I recently read about his alleged involvement in a housing scandal, it brought back memories. Mr. Thomas was a social studies teacher who was pursuing his law degree in the evening. He vowed to leave the teaching profession as soon as he passed the bar. Thomas was one of many pedagogues who had a traveling program.

Since the school was overcrowded, it was virtually impossible for any teacher to retain one room for the entire day. Therefore, most of us had to scurry around the building schlepping materials from one floor to another within the parameters of the bell schedule. Often, the class arrived before the teacher, creating a slue of problems.

In order to cope with this situation, you had to prepare rexographed sheets with a warm-up or do-now assignment. If not, then you quickly had to erase the board and commence writing something new and fast. Most teachers are aware that you must engage the average class instantly or you're in big trouble. Mr. Thomas would have none of that. While most teachers were running to various classrooms, Thomas would saunter on by using his infamous Chaplinesque shuffle step. He was a comedian by nature and used to entertain daily in the teachers' room.

Upon arriving to his class, *New York Times* tucked firmly under his arm, Thomas did not seem to be in quite a hurry to erase the board and begin his lesson. Why should he?

Mr. Thomas had discovered the perfect solution to this traveling madness. Whatever lesson was left on the board by the previous teacher was his lesson for that particular period. It made no difference that he taught social studies. If a mathematics or Spanish lesson were available, then that was his lesson for the period. I wonder what he did if the board were empty or what he said to his students when they complained that he was teaching the wrong subject.

Ironically, his argumentative nature, which led him into legal profession, would eventually cause his demise. Approximately twenty years after leaving teaching, the profession had changed, but apparently he had not. He was accused of traveling to housing court judges with bribes for his tenant clients.

The traveling man had taken the "easy" way out again. Perhaps if he'd been reprimanded for his offenses way back when, these allegations of impropriety may not have occurred.

Nevertheless, Mr. Thomas, former teacher and disgraced lawyer, will have to travel yet another path in his next venue.

BITING THE HAND THAT FEEDS HIM

Mr. Kirk, who arrived in the late 80s as a math teacher, gave new meaning to the absent-minded professor syndrome. He lasted one year, which really surprised us. We couldn't fathom how he survived even a single day.

Mr. Kirk was really bizarre. Whenever he encountered a stressful situation, and there were many, he'd begin biting his wrist and worked his way up his arm. He managed to chew his way up to the elbow until he reached the funny bone. We used to ask, was it a two-, three-, or four-elbow day, Mr. K? Furthermore, to relieve his frustration during preparation time, one could find him sitting or standing snugly in the teacher's closet. One could only imagine what questions the former sitting college instructor would be asked when he emerged from the closet.

Kirk also had a penchant to be extremely forgetful. He would often leave his magnetic copying card in the Xerox machine. This card automatically recorded the limited number of copies teachers could make during the year. Who knows how many unscrupulous teachers used his "Discover card" for their own purposes. One day I even found his jacket on top of the machine. When I returned his card, which was inside the machine, he asked me where I found them. I replied that your coat was inside the Xerox and the card was on top. He shrugged his shoulders, scratched his head, and walked away.

My next encounter with Kirk occurred when I asked for the results of the school-wide October math exam. Incredulously, he responded, "What exam?" Then, he stopped and thought for a moment and added, "I never received them." Six months later, after the "post test" was administered, I returned to his room to collect the examinations and results. He calmly handed me the papers and results from October.

Later that year, during statewide exams, Kirk was proctoring an eighth grade class on the fifth floor. When I entered the room to collect the materials in my role as testing coordinator, I noticed that the students apparently taped a "KICK ME" sign on his rear pants pocket. An open condom was protruding from the same pocket.

Soon, Kirk stories began to circulate throughout the building. One incident, which he corroborated, was the time he was locked out of another school in the middle of winter without a coat. He remembered that he had left his car keys in an unlocked car and thought he'd be gone for just a moment. When he attempted to reenter the building, the door was locked. After twenty minutes of pounding, Kirk was beside himself, shivering. Suddenly, a hobo strolling by noticed his predicament. He pressed the bell and instantly the door opened. The school authorities probably should have let the tramp in.

I wonder what planet Mr. K is on now. Perhaps, one day, with his credentials, he'll resurface as superintendent or chancellor of the school system.

Much Ado
About Nothing

Upon the arrival from England, G took the school by storm. This teacher had the cure for what was ailing us: Will (Shakespeare). Don't misunderstand me. The concept, though not unique, was an excellent one. Shakespeare, however, became the panacea for every facet of teaching and all the students' problems. One might refer to G's teaching as "Everything Shakespeare."

Even though many students enjoyed the program, they couldn't stand the demands being made on them. G appeared to be well meaning and even emitted artsy airs, but we knew better. You would only be recognized if you could perform some service for G. On the other hand, G rarely, if ever, listened to what you were saying. He always had a retort that when in this particular place or school, it was done better. The implication was that G was the reason for success.

One year G took credit as the teacher who "held up the school" because the students' reading scores in his classes went down one tenth of a point less than the rest of the classes in the school. This reminds of a politician's claim that he was responsible for safe streets because the increase in crime actually decreased. The following year, when his classes' scores plummeted, G was on the outs with the administration. Who was going to help G in his time of need? Good ol' Will of course. He'd always come through in the past.

Didn't Will help G pass the grueling NTE Exam? Wasn't the bard's work great for school presentations? Even the great William Shakespeare could not save him this time.

The students, who should have loved and admired G's Shakespearian fanaticism, showed their lack of appreciation by bombarding him with books, papers, tomatoes, and spit balls while turning around to write notes on the blackboard. Things got so bad that G was mercilessly booed off the stage during his students' performance of *Much Ado About Nothing*.

People attempted to assist, but there was a refusal to listen. It seemed as if he were the "King of Denial." G even refused to allow traveling teachers to use his room, despite their being required to hold classes there. Furthermore, other teachers were falsely accused of destroying and defacing property in G's classroom. Once, G stated that since he had an important conference with a college intern scheduled, I would have to relocate my class for two periods.

Eventually G was forced to resign and seek employment elsewhere. Did G's syllabus and delusions of grandeur result in the ultimate Shakespearian tragedy?

KIDNAPPED

Educationally speaking, kidnapping conjures up thoughts of youngsters being abducted by strangers on their way to school or by an estranged parent from within the school. However, have you ever heard of an entire class that was kidnapped? And for profit?

These "kidnappings" transpired in the 1970s for what is known in the trade as coverage credit. When a teacher is absent and a substitute is unavailable, a teacher on staff picks up an extra period for compensation, which is called a coverage. Historically, many teachers abhor coverages because they don't know most of the students and have little control over them. Some even call it "blood money." Yet there are pedagogues in every school who desire or need coverages to supplement their income. These teachers generally view it as a second job and often volunteer for as many coverages as they can get.

Mr. Selden and Mr. Rossini used to engage in contests as to who could get the most coverages. There were times when a class remained uncovered and Selden and Rossini, if free that period, would race to the room and volunteer their services for that coveted coverage credit.

One time, Mr. R. noticed an uncovered class standing outside their room with no teacher in the immediate area. Mr.

S. also saw a class "wandering" the halls in search of their teacher. Rossini took one class to his room and Selden "hijacked" or kidnapped the other class for credit.

How do classes get uncovered? There may have been a clerical error or the potential covering teacher may have arrived late. Perhaps the covering teacher never received the proper notification or maybe a note was left on the door for the teacher or class to report to another room and somehow the note disappeared. At any rate, the two made a practice of kidnapping classes for pay and boasted about it. One time, another teacher "covered" her own class for extra pay because when she was relieved of her regular assignment, the covering teacher took ill and she had to return to her classroom.

Things like this should not happen, but in an imperfect world, they do. So, if you are ever looking for a class and cannot locate them, look for teachers like Rossini and Selden and you'll probably find them.

LOST IN THE CITY

You would think that going on an educational excursion would be fun, wouldn't you? Here are some cases in point.

One spring day in the 1970s, I went on a class trip with Mr. Jackson and Mr. Raymond. At one point as we toured the city, the three classes stopped for a rest in the park. Mr. Raymond decided to remain there while Mr. Jackson and I visited the wondrous sights. On the way home, we sighted Mr. Raymond on the train station. He was alone! When we asked where his class was, he simply shrugged his shoulders.

We later discovered that Mr. R. had fallen asleep on a park bench. After a brief snooze, he awoke to find himself alone. What happened to the students? Several were arrested for fare beating and some were attacked by students from another school. The rest, somehow, managed to return home without incident.

Mercury Man also had a trip to remember. It seemed as though a student who failed to bring the required consent slip illegally followed the class on a trip downtown. On the way back, he unscrewed a light bulb on the train and threw it on the track, causing sparks and disruption in service.

The train came to a grinding halt and the police entered and attempted to arrest the perpetrator. "Marvelous

Mercury" vigorously protested, so much so that the police issued him a summons for disorderly conduct, primarily because they couldn't comprehend most of what he was saying.

Mercury knew he had done nothing wrong. Therefore, he canvassed the neighborhood to round up character witnesses as well as eyewitnesses to fight this injustice. When all appeared in court, they were advised that it was just a hearing to plead. Another loss for Mercury Man.

A fun trip for sixth graders was taken by Mrs. Leon, Mrs. Sherman, and Mr. Carlton. They were supposed to visit a suburban amusement park, but the buses failed to appear. That did not deter them. They decided to use public transportation.

At the park, they parted and went their separate ways. Later, the female teachers noticed what appeared to them to be a homeless man, covered with newspapers, sleeping in the grass. Feeling sorry for him, they offered a sandwich and cup of coffee. Startled at the offer, Mr. Carlton, their colleague, awoke and stated that he had already eaten.

By four o'clock, anxious parents were calling the school to find out why the classes had not yet returned from the trip. There was no contact and nobody knew where they were except the suburban bus drivers who drove them back and forth on the same route five or six times. It seemed as though the teachers, all from the immediate area, knew the "best way" to get home via public transportation. They arrived at the school at 7 p.m.

At the beginning of my career, I went with a veteran, Mr. Ipp, to the Statue of Liberty. When it was time to depart, we took a head count and discovered to our dismay that two students were "missing." We decided to look for them while the others boarded the boat to Battery Park. We soon realized that the two were already on the boat. However, the boat was filled to capacity and we were not allowed on. I was nervous. Two unescorted classes at Battery Park. Should we call the police? Mr. Ipp calmed my nerves by telling me not to worry. "They'll be there." As we alighted one half hour later, sure enough, Mr. Ipp was correct.

TWO FOR THE LOGE

When VCRs, cable, and viewing home movies became fashionable, the principal decided to reward student attendance by showing a movie of the month for those deserving students who were absent three days or less. However, there was a nominal charge for students who were absent a day or more, while those who had perfect attendance went gratis.

The principal was always present when the teachers escorted their classes to the movie room, most likely to collect the money. One day, Mr. Michaels, an administrative assistant, was in his stead. At the end of the day we could see the principal shaking Mr. Michael's pockets for loose change while holding him in an upside-down position.

Even in the old days, showing films was considered educational and was used to the hilt by some pedagogues. Mr. Howard and Mr. Greenstein used to combine classes every Friday afternoon for a viewing. The classes were motivated, quiet, and receptive to this type of alternative education. Soon, the films were shown on a more frequent basis. When the administration got wind of this, both teachers received a letter stating that they should avoid showing too many films, lest the students get "cinema eyes."

Mr. Grossman, an assistant principal, was aware of this from the onset. One day he discovered two students from Mr. Howard's class in the hallway without a pass. Since it was Friday afternoon, Mr. Grossman approached the darkened room, knocked on the door, and politely stated, "Two for the Loge."

KEEP TALKING

Have you ever seen a person on the street talking to himself? What did you think? Was he crazy or just like you and me? The reason I bring this up is that four former staffers—Mr. B., Mrs. J., Ms. S., and Ms. T.—had the unusual gift of gab, which could drive some people stark raving mad.

The...er...a..."four" mentioned people were so talkative that it would not be uncommon to walk past them and see them engaged in conversation with themselves. It didn't take long to surmise that the previous listener had walked or ran away. That did not deter them. The conversation must continue, regardless of who was or wasn't listening was their motto. At times a new person would arrive and continue the prior conversation in midstream. And, the conversation was so one-sided that you could never get a word in. You often felt like plugging up your ears with cotton, or just screaming.

The four should have entered the old television game show *Keep Talking* as an entry. If not, they should have formed a coalition as union representatives to try and talk the principal out of or into something. They probably could have talked him out of the school or pull out the few remaining hairs he had left.

The conversation with any of them would generally culminate with a repetition of their life story. They repeated these stories so often that they eventually became anecdotes in their teaching styles. In order to avoid hearing the same discourse daily, teachers used to run by feigning some illness, important errand, or bathroom emergency. Those who weren't so observant were caught in the web of the endless speech and sermon. Once, two teachers conversing in the office spotted two of them coming in their direction. What could they do? Without a word, the two teachers picked up telephones and began an imaginary conversation to avoid the hundredth rendition of their life story.

The gang of four would stop at nothing to engage someone in their banter. Whether they corralled someone during lunch, on a prep period, in the bathroom, or at a bus stop, the talk was the thing. I once spotted one of the four chasing a moving vehicle down the street to make a point to the car or its occupant; I'm not sure which.

Funny that you never saw them speak to each other. Perhaps they knew of their impending part-time listening status. Students in their classes would roll their eyes as they exited, hoping that one of them would not be next on the schedule.

Speaking is an integral part of teaching. How does the teacher know if the point is getting across if she does not listen and gets no feedback?

ABSENT-MINDED PROFESSORS

In the course of the day, it is really easy to misplace something of value, either personal or work related. That's because many teachers travel to different rooms for instruction and eventually visit various offices in the building throughout the day. Misplaced items include roll books, marking books, textbooks, notices, and student papers.

In some cases we've heard, "My pocketbook is gone." Somehow, students occasionally are able to infiltrate locked closets and pilfer personal belongings of teachers and fellow students. Two teachers had their pocketbooks swiped twice in one week. A gentleman had his wallet lifted just after cashing his check.

Sometimes you have something in your hand one minute and because of the many distractions that occur, sometimes you are unable to locate it. This brings me to Ms. Buford, an affable young woman, who had a penchant for forgetfulness. I've learned to make multiple copies of whatever I disseminate because ten seconds later Buford can't remember where or what it was you gave her or that you were ever there. Aware of her shortcoming, Ms. B. assigned students to remind her where she placed tests, report cards, circulars, record cards, and other assorted handouts. She trained them to show staffers on what shelf or in what drawer the item of question was in.

Invariably, Buford's report cards, collected quarterly, were missing. She'd wander into an AP's office and innocently ask, "Did you see my report cards?" The AP commented that he had them at one time, but returned them several days ago. She had to turn the room upside down for days in order to find them in spite of the monitor's help. This happened because the student rememberer was not present when she placed the report cards in her top drawer, the last place she looked. Prior to discovering them, she filled out a duplicate set.

She's not the only one with instant memory loss. Ms. Franks, the "media specialist," usually needs four or more notices to follow through on most things. She laughs and states how could she be so absent-minded upon receiving the fifth notice.

The teacher in a previous chapter "Biting the Hand that Feeds Him" was a perfect example of the absent-minded professor. He returned the first exam results, which he "never received," instead of the second set, which he also never saw.

YELLING THEATER
IN A CROWDED FIRE

O ur school has been involved in fires, bomb scares, floods, stabbings, assaults, shootings, stonings, stampedes, wilding incidents, and accidental deaths and injuries over my thirty-four years of employment. At least annually, there has been an evacuation due to a major crisis.

In the early 1970s a student torched five rooms in less than a year. What was his penalty? Two meager suspensions! We also probably encountered more false alarms than half the city. At one time the school's theme song was "The Bells Are Ringing." Eventually, someone had the bright idea to paint red dye on all the fire alarms in the school. This successful strategy enabled the perpetrator to be caught "red-handed."

In the late 80s a major fire occurred in the science laboratory due to a chemical explosion. Most teachers quickly escorted their classes to safety as practiced during fire drills. However, a few staffers panicked and ran away from their charges. Two teachers even took their groups to the site of the conflagration instead of evacuating the building, a sort of dangerous show and tell.

The principal was absolutely furious at what transpired. He ordered everyone to wait outside and not leave the school grounds until he met with them. Mrs. Spooner would not hear of it. She had to report to her after school employment and nothing was going to stop her. Seeing her try to leave, a security guard leaped on her vehicle to prevent her egress. A good Samaritan passing by erroneously assumed a carjacking in progress and attacked the guard. Spooner nearly ran them both over as she burned rubber exiting the school yard.

In the early 1990s a small fire brought disastrous results. The entire building filled up with smoke. Three teachers were hospitalized for smoke inhalation, while the rest of the school body thought they escaped safely. Once outside the terror seemed worse than the fire. Teenage truants were across the street on a sixth-floor roof and bombarded us with huge bricks for several minutes as we raced back toward the school area. Two students were grazed and were slightly injured. The police were notified, but were too late to apprehend the brick throwers. Were we in the Middle East?

We've also had numerous bomb scares, but the only time an actual bomb-like device was discovered in the building no call was received. A security guard spotted the device on the first floor. The bomb squad investigated and removed the device as we froze on the snow-covered streets for nearly two hours. We later heard it was a dud, but many of us were skeptical.

These unbelievable crises would make for great theater, but unfortunately, this is reality.

PASS OUT, QUIETLY

As a freshman college student, whenever the bell rang to signal the end of the period, a particular professor used to say, "Pass out quietly." About half the class did not recognize any humor in this double entendre. Why do I mention this? It just so happened that year during the change of periods two teachers passed out, but not so quietly.

Mrs. Sterling, a veteran teacher, had a medical problem for quite some time. Doctors were at a loss to explain why she passed out so frequently.

One morning as the students were exiting her room, Mrs. Sterling was accidentally knocked in the head. She entered the hallway feeling a bit dizzy from the contact. Mr. Jones, the Dean of Students, noticed her unsteadiness and raced to her assistance. By the time he reached her she was semiconscious and on her way down. Jones caught the full weight of her limp body, which propelled him into the wall, whereupon he hit his head, sending him to the land of unconsciousness.

The two bodies lay motionless in the hallway. Emergency services was called immediately, but did not arrive in a timely fashion. The principal suspended departmental until further notice without explanation.

It must have taken about forty-five minutes before the EMS arrived, but it seemed like an eternity. Most of the staff and students could only speculate why they had to remain in their rooms. To explain publicly may have sent shock, panic, and thrill-seeking waves through the school. Thankfully, both teachers eventually returned to work.

Over the years there have been several incidents of students and staff collapsing, but it was usually do to asthma or some sports-related injury. This incident was unique because they passed out almost simultaneously in each other's arms.

II

ADMINISTRATIVE GAFFES

THE GIANT

One spring day in 1971 screams of "There's a giant in the schoolyard," pervaded the halls of the school. My immediate reaction was could it be New York Giant quarterback, Fran Tarkenton, who happened to be involved in a district reading program? Perhaps it was Willie Mays, my boyhood idol as a New York Giant, who was now visiting Shea Stadium with the San Francisco Giants. Suddenly, I heard screaming that there's a ten-foot giant in the schoolyard and they're throwing bricks at him. My interest piqued.

Not convinced, I still thought that they were referring to a muscular physical education teacher who was about six feet nine inches tall. When I asked a veteran colleague about the situation, he laughed and assured me that the kids were not lying; there was a giant in the yard.

Who was this giant? He was Eddie, the giant from Ringling Brothers Circus, who just happened to live across the street from the school. Naively, he entered the yard at lunchtime and the students went berserk. They immediately deemed him to be some kind of monster and bombarded him with rocks, bottles, bricks, and sticks until he was chased out of the area.

When the principal heard about this incident, he immediately went on the public address system, filibustering for twenty minutes about how wrong it was to harm him or any other person. Furthermore, he added about fifteen times, that the man is a human being and should not be referred to as the giant.

At the close of his long-winded sermon, the principal proudly stated that the school was going to have a special guest at next week's assembly program. He said, "The giant is going to visit and speak to you."

HALF-TRUTHS GO MARCHING ON

Wow, brilliant, and that makes sense were some of the remarks we often heard about the principal's response to a particular problem. We later discovered to our chagrin that Mr. Wendell was a master of deception. He always had a hidden agenda coupled with an educationally sound reason for implementing any plan or idea. On the surface, how could anyone argue?

One year it was decided that the sixth graders would do better academically if they remained in their homeroom all day. Therefore, the longstanding departmental policy was dropped for grade six. The self-contained classroom concept lasted for three years. No reason was offered for the reinstatement of full-scale traveling. Curiously, at that time, Mr. Wendell had relegated a former physical education teacher who possessed a general elementary school license to the self-contained sixth grade, hoping that she'd transfer. After three years of torment she left and so did the self-contained sixth grade.

Wendell always advised the faculty that he welcomed grievances against oversized classes. But when you filed one, he'd call you down and intimidate you from seeking further redress. One complaining pedagogue reminded him that we were encouraged to file these types of grievances. The principal countered that he really didn't mean it. What he probably meant to say was don't file them against him or the administration.

Mr. Wendell was a powerful, determined, and aggressive individual, not one to be reckoned with.

Furthermore, he demanded unconditional loyalty from his staff, but gave little in return. His unwritten philosophy appeared to be "what can you do for me tomorrow?"

To add insult to injury, he chided staffers for being absent the day before and or after long weekends and holidays. As he did this, his chauffeurs were preparing the limo for his early drive to the airport. If you got in his way or disagreed with him, he'd devise a plan to get revenge, even if it meant changing your program and duties at anytime during the year. He ran the school as his personal fiefdom. Anyone who challenged him was tormented, dismissed, or transferred.

Mr. W often used students to spy on selected teachers. If he didn't like the teacher or suspected something was amiss, he would encourage pupils to write detailed accounts about that person. Once, a teacher was accused of making nasty remarks about Wendell as he left the room. The teacher sat in the office for the next six months doing clerical work until she transferred. He then called the principal of her new school advising him of the prize package he was about to receive. He also telephoned physicians to challenge diagnoses about employees who were ill or injured in the line of duty.

After his retirement, he became a substitute teacher at a nearby high school without much success. The fact that he castigated teachers for not being able to control classes did not phase him when he was unable to do so. Six months later at his retirement party, comments about his tactics were nixed by the current administration. Was it so bad an opening line that "There's no substitute for a good principal; or is it, there's no principal who's a good substitute?"

There was even a resemblance to President Lincoln. Lincoln walked several miles in the snow to return money, while Wendell did the same to save wear and tear on his automobile. Lincoln was a rail-splitter; Wendell was a hair-splitter. Honest Abe ended the Civil War while Wendell initiated many civil wars between colleagues during his divide-and-conquer reign. His half-truths go marching on.

CLOUDS IN HIS COFFEE

Mr. Lester was an affable fellow who took pride in his role as assistant principal. He was one of the few administrators who unconditionally backed up teachers in times of distress. Mr. Lester expected the same loyalty, but never received it, especially from his fellow administrators.

The reason for this lack of kinship was that he rarely wrote up teachers for being out of line. He preferred the humane and rational approach of speaking to the teachers and working out the problem. While the principal and other assistants were constantly typing nasty and petty letters for the file, Lester would not cave in. He was too busy assisting students, teachers, and other staff members. He would not concern himself or be bothered with denigrating pedagogues and their morale. The opinion among his colleagues that he wasn't tough enough relegated him to the status of doing menial tasks. Fed up with what he believed to be an unequal voice in school policy, Lester often lamented, "What am I, an errand boy?"

When he wasn't helping people, Mr. Lester could be seen coffee mug in hand, drawing at his desk. An accomplished artist, he drew many designs and pictures for school advertisements. One of his pet doodles was sketching clouds of all shapes and sizes. They encircled almost of his official and unofficial art work. Mr. L. would have had "clouds in his coffee," but he wasn't so vain.

He often felt disillusioned and depressed about his standing among his peers. This made him prone to occasional fits of anger and loud outbursts. You could hear his "Hey you" from one end of the floor to the other or "I've had it," with the door slamming behind him. He also went berserk when the Bullshit stamp (a future chapter) was planted on his prized Indian Head and when his automobile was stolen by a seventh grader while parked in front of the school.

He overcame his tantrums rather quickly and returned to being the truly nice guy he really was. He refused to yield to the evil demands of the administration about "getting" certain teachers. Lester just wanted the best for everyone. The teachers loved and respected him for it, but he suffered because he was often left out of his colleagues' secret meetings.

Mr. L. was also a very funny individual who enjoyed joking with staff members. On the other hand, he was also the butt of others' mockery concerning his "errand boy status." One day, while the district superintendent was touring the building, Lester noticed a door opening at the first bell. He took off like a bolt of lightning from one of his clouds and leaped on top of the class as they attempted an early emergence. A roar of "Get back in there" could be heard three floors away.

That was Mr. Lester; just doing his job the best way he knew.

THE WON TON
SOUP REBELLION

The most dreaded chore in teaching is one that has absolutely nothing to do with it—lunch duty. Every second or third year the homeroom teacher was required to serve several periods of cafeteria duty each week. Quota teachers (those not having official classes) had this task every year. You have to make sure that no student runs upstairs or outside and prevent fights (physical or food), all in a scene of bedlam. At the end of a typical lunch period, your head and ears are ringing from the noise. It's noisier than most airports during takeoffs and touchdowns. If you're lucky enough, you can get outside lunch duty. That's terrific in warm weather, but have you ever stayed outside with the wind chill of thirty below or get pelted by snow or ice? Once it was too cold for me to remain outside. The administrator on duty remarked that he didn't see me today. My response was that I didn't see him either.

I'm not arguing the importance of student safety during lunch, particularly in schools where students are permitted to leave the grounds and return to play in the school yard. However, this is not what most educators had in mind when they entered the profession. Currently, this abhorrent task has contractually ended for teachers, but administrators, school aides, and security officers have taken up the slack.

One lunch duty tale I'd like to relate is the time when Miss White, the lunchroom supervisor, scolded a teacher for eating won ton soup while on patrol. She berated him in front of the faculty and students for not devoting his complete attention to his assignment. She also informed the principal and a letter was written for his file. The young, inexperienced teacher was totally embarrassed and at a loss for words. The rest of the faculty on patrol, seeing what transpired, consoled their colleague and devised a plan of retribution.

The next day when Miss White was supervising the cafeteria, she walked outside and gasped in disbelief. There she saw twelve teachers on patrol, all eating won ton soup. She rolled her eyes, threw her hands up in the air, and left the scene hurriedly with out a word. Perhaps she went to buy some soup.

The point of the story is that White should have spoken to the teacher privately about the matter. Then, all would have probably been forgotten. But, in this great educational system of ours, the modus operandi in many schools is shoot first and ask questions later.

THE OFFICE

If you took a look inside Mrs. Berman's office, you'd be amazed how it resembled Noah's Ark. There were two or more of everything imaginable. Lord only knows where she obtained these items. How Mrs. B. ever found anything was even more amazing. Yet she claimed that she knew where everything was, a sort of organized chaos.

Mrs. Berman was a long-time assistant principal who had a penchant for working on multiple tasks simultaneously. She was involved in English, reading, guidance, testing, programming, and special education. Her office was constantly filled (with people and papers) and the phone was always ringing off the hook. There was Mrs. B., in the middle of it all. It looked impossible, but somehow positive results were achieved for the most part.

Before Berman could finish one thought, the phone rang or another person would enter causing further disruption. How could one cope with constant interruptions and work effectively? It's no wonder that her home shopping list once arrived at a local high school instead of the names of the students who were promoted there. It was also rumored that student record cards were hidden in the trunk of her automobile.

If you had a pre- or post-observation conference, it had to be continued next time due to constant interruptions. Ultimately, many conferences concerning observed lessons were never completed. We had a standing joke that there was a statue of limitations of twenty-five years on discussing and receiving a written document regarding an observed lesson. I soon learned to bring paperwork with me every time I had to see her because I surmised that for the forty-five minutes I'd be there, we'd be fortunate to get in five quality minutes due to constant interruptions. Nevertheless, Mrs. B. happened to be an extremely bright woman who was compassionate toward staff and students. She never let the mess in her office mess up her mind.

One day we learned that a district observation team was arriving on Monday. On Friday, the principal strongly encouraged Berman to come in on the weekend and redecorate. After many hours, the office finally looked presentable (due to her husband's help), only to return to its previous look in a few days.

Occasionally, if you looked out the window, you'd see someone parking her car for her. There was a designated parker on call because Berman had difficulty with parallel parking. Her driving skills had left a lot to be desired too. If you saw a car weaving all over the road creating hundreds of near collisions, it was probably the Berman mobile en route to her place of employment.

I never looked inside her car, but if it were anything like her office...

TAKING OVER THE CLASS

During my early years, the principal, Mr. Weissman, had an excellent idea. He'd tour the building, open a door at random, and continue whatever lesson you were teaching. The only problem was that more often than not, catastrophes occurred when this happened.

One day Mr. Weissman entered the room and took over the lesson as usual. This time, a seventh grader named Rodney ran up to the principal requesting permission to leave the room. Mr. W. was standing near the door and said no. Rodney said, "Get out of my way, bro," and shoved him lightly on his way out. Weissman was astounded. He shook his head and quietly left the room. What chance does the classroom teacher have if this happens to the principal?

Another time he entered in the midst of my teaching a most difficult class. This time, instead of immediately taking over the lesson, Weisman walked around the room observing students' notebooks. As he neared the clothing closet, Frankie, who was hiding in the closet, heard footsteps. Quickly the door opened, and Frankie shouted, "Boo!" The startled principal jumped back in fright and turned to Frankie. "Do you do this sort of thing at home, young man?"

he asked. When Frankie responded in the affirmative, Mr. W. led him back to the closet, closed the door, and left the room.

During another "takeover" the lesson was not going particularly well. Weissman told the class to stop what they were doing and stretch. One student, an habitual truant, except for today, stretched a bit too far, fell off his chair, and was rushed to the hospital after striking his head on the leg of a piano. I wonder what lesson he learned today about attending class.

We were always on the lookout for Mr. Weissman, never knowing when he'd appear in your room. I remember completing a lesson one minute early. Should I continue, review, start something new, or ask additional questions, I pondered. I decided not to do any of the above, bearing in mind that Weissman never stops in with less than a minute remaining. Sure enough, with thirty seconds left, Mr. W. arrived, wanting to know what was going on. I explained my position and showed him the work and worksheets.

After that episode, I never ended a lesson even one second early. In comparing notes with other colleagues, I learned of similar experiences. Mr. Weissman's concept of unannounced visitations and attempting to teach each class was commendable. Yet, somehow, due to a variety of misadventures, its overall effect was less than enlightening.

LOST WEEKEND

An educational administrators' weekend at an upstate resort sounds like fun, doesn't it? A recipe for disaster would be the more appropriate terminology.

Our principal, Mr. Jarvis, and his long-time assistant jubilantly drove to the resort for a weekend of thrills, so they thought. Why not get a head start and leave Friday morning? they both agreed. It didn't matter that the principals' conference was on Jarvis' schedule that morning. After all, Mr. Paulson would attend in Jarvis' stead, wearing the proper name tag and taping the entire conference. Mr. Green would then deliver the tape by placing it in the principal's barbecue pit. A real CIA operation was in progress.

That afternoon, the administrators were engaged in a round of golf. Suddenly, the assistant principal somehow lost control of his golf cart and sailed wildly downhill. "Look out!" he screamed as the principal, back towards him, was about to enter his own cart. Too late! He struck Jarvis, causing him to break his right arm and left leg.

From that point on, Mr. Borden, Jarvis' buddy and trusted associate for over twenty-five years, was persona non grata and eventually transferred to another school. Apparently, the principal never forgave his "former best friend."

To add insult to injury, the conference tape malfunctioned. Have we all learned a lesson?

By the way, if you ever run into Mr. Borden, or if he runs into you, ask him if he ever passed his golf cart driving test.

WHAT'S IN A NAME?

The most prestigious event in junior high school is the eighth-grade graduation. The school has had ceremonies in movie theaters, high schools, colleges, and even its own auditorium. Teachers of graduating seniors usually attend the pomp and circumstance. Prior to the festivities students, parents, and teachers are given explicit travel directions to the graduation site via public and private transportation at least two weeks in advance. Colleagues often make arrangements to meet and travel in a group.

One year the graduation was to be held at Lehman High School, which is located in the East Tremont section of the Bronx. When someone would ask where the graduation would be held that year, the typical response was Lehman, dropping the high school part of it. How do you get there? people would ask. Two days before the ceremony I overheard queries such as, is the graduation at Lehman? What time? How do you get there?

On that fateful morning, Mrs. Pringle, a teacher, arrived at Lehman extremely early in order to get a decent parking space. After wandering around for twenty minutes she began to worry. Where was everyone? She did not recognize anyone. Did she get the time wrong? Just as she was about to call the school, two other teachers and the assistant principal in charge of the graduation entered the parking lot. Thank God, thought Mrs. P., but where was everyone else? The three greeted her and asked where the students were. After all, commencement was at 10 a.m. and it was almost nine thirty. One teacher decided to call the school. A secretary answered and as soon as soon as she heard the word graduation, she said Lehman High School on Tremont Avenue.

The teacher gasped and looked incredulously at her colleagues. "The graduation is at Lehman High School!" she screamed. They were standing on the campus of Lehamn College! They all looked at each other in disbelief. "Who knows how to get to Lehman High School?" one inquired. "I think I do," responded another. The third one offered, "Perhaps we should call the school again and ask for directions." "Are you crazy?" said the AP. "I'm in charge of the whole thing and I don't even know how to get there. How embarrassing!"

Suddenly the cars were speeding across the Bronx in search of Lehman High School. After several wrong turns and getting misinformation about their final destination, the geniuses finally arrived about forty-five minutes late. When they asked a local resident if this was Lehman, the response was that Lehman College was in the West Bronx.

Students were never told the reason for the hour delay. At the podium, the assistant principal welcomed parents, students, teachers, and distinguished guests to Lehman College.

THE BULLSHIT STAMP

What do the principal's timecard, hundreds of memos, an Indian head, and toilet bowls have in common? Just look at the title of the chapter.

It seemed as though one or more disgruntled and/or mischievous employees were so fed up with the constant flow of paper that was deemed wasteful that they decided it was all BS. As a result, a stamp was purchased to etch their feelings. Initially it was used on all official documents that were posted and disseminated among the staff. People were smirking in various corners of the building discussing the latest episode of the stamp, while administrators fumed and sent out spies to catch the perpetrators. To the powers that be, this was the most important segment of the school day.

As time went on, no one had a clue about who was involved. To make it even more difficult for detection, the stampers would take an occasional hiatus. Yet, just when you thought it was over, the infamous stamp appeared in the most amazing and obscure places. One day the principal was unable to locate his timecard. After an exhaustive search, his card was discovered in the women's bathroom with BS stamped all over it. The next day an assistant principal's card was found in the men's room similarly decorated. Was there a conspiracy?

The next time I entered the men's bathroom, I noticed that the stamp was used in the deepest bowels of the toilet. It was also visible on doors, walls, closets, bulletin boards, and various memorandums hanging throughout the school. Apparently, the memos and mundane targets were not enough. They had outlived their usefulness and greater ones were on the horizon.

One day an assistant principal returned to his office to find his prized Indian head the victim of the BS stamp. The stamper(s) had ruined its proud forehead. The AP stormed out of his office vowing to get whoever did this. Fifteen years later, upon his retirement, I don't think that he or anyone else really knew who committed the acts, although speculation pointed to a group of insurrectionist teachers.

If the administration had spent as much time educating the children, perhaps the math and reading test scores might have been higher.

Who knows? Perhaps one day, the stamp might return updated as BS II, Son of BS the movie, or BS Revisited because as you read this, the endless flow of paper and memos continue.

THE SIXTH
TEACHER

Early in my career I was assigned a third grade language arts cluster position.

This means that I was to instruct four third grade reading and English classes during the regular teacher's preparation period. All the classes responded extremely well and I felt confident and good about what I was doing. Little did I realize what was in store.

My colleague and friend, Mr. Marshall, was having an extremely difficult time with his fourth grade class. My reward for being successful was to inherit his class as a result of administrative moves necessitated by the November retirement of a veteran teacher. Frankly, I did not fare much better as the second teacher of that particular group. At times, the class behaved somewhat decently and learned.

However, too often, the situation was chaotic. I had to resort to barricading the door with my desk to prevent a group of nine-year-olds from running out of the room. One child simply refused to walk on the floor in the classroom. Fidel would jump or leap from desk to desk or desk to closet. Andres responded that the devil made him do whatever wrong he had done while Jose blamed all of his misfortunes on his nonexistent twin brother.

One spring day I made the mistake of escorting them to the schoolyard for recreation. Before I could say class 406, they ran away in all different directions. There I was, standing alone, a relatively new teacher, wondering what happened, where they were, and what to do about it. What if someone got hit by a car, kidnapped, or worse? What was I to do?

I was still naïve enough not to report the incident hoping that somehow they would all return safely in time. I went up to my room and waited. Within fifteen minutes, they miraculously returned safely. Naturally this was the first and last recess of the year.

Looking back, if this occurred today, I'd probably have a coronary.

As time marched on conditions deteriorated. I was losing control and requested another assignment. Teachers three, four, and five didn't fare much better. However, teacher number six seemed to possess magical powers. He arrived in April and almost immediately the class was transformed into a well-behaved group that worked all day without incident. The administration considered Mr. Hagen a fabulous teacher simply because he kept them quiet, in the room, and actively working. What was his secret?

Hagen confided in me that the class was copying their basal reader from cover to cover all day, every day. How simplistic! Why didn't I think of that? Is that what education is about? Perhaps they were learning. Maybe it was a survival technique.

Nevertheless, the class was under control and Mr. Hagen was a genius and savior.

In retrospect, I don't think I could have followed through with Hagen's system even if I thought of it. It just wasn't me. If you think that such classes don't exist today, you are dead wrong. There are many schools that go through several teachers each year.

The public has no idea of how often this situation recurs.

III

BUREAUCRATIC
BUNGLING

THE IRVING CLASS

This class was way ahead of its time. Long before special education, alternative schools, magnet programs, and academies were in vogue, there was a special class for students at risk. The urban class had an enrollment of fifteen. Students with nicknames such as Rockhead, Scooter, and the Judge are indicative that they were forerunners of gangsta rappers. They were a self-contained group that had a strict, father figure-type of instructor and a full-time aide. The class was tucked away in a corner of the building without much fanfare.

Since being self-contained is not foolproof, occasionally students would wander the halls and create a bit of mayhem. It didn't take long for the rest of the student population to fear the students from this particular class. As students talked, the urban class acts of horror increased one hundred fold. By midyear the monster had been created. Everyone, teachers included, feared having any contact with them or even going near their room.

When asked what class they were in, the students mumbled urban class, which evolved into the "Irving Class." The students who misbehaved in regular classes were then threatened with sitting in the urban class for the rest of the day. The unruly students would often reply, "I'm not going to the Irving Class."

By today's standards, the urban students were rather meek. However, folklore has a way of raising things to a grandiose scale.

I wonder where the Judge, Rockhead, Scooter, and the rest of the urban clan are now.

I also wonder if they, or anyone else, realize that many classes in the general education population of today's urban schools are, in reality, Irving-type classes.

Brrr...Baby, It's Cold Inside

When listening to winter weather reports many people are concerned with the wind-chill factor. This enables them to determine what kind and how many layers of clothing to wear. Would you believe that there was a wind-chill factor at times inside many of our classrooms during the winter months? If you were a nonbeliever, then one look inside the school auditorium would have made you a true believer.

Wearing hats, gloves, winter coats, sweaters, thermal underwear, and two pairs of socks were the order of the day for many years during scheduled assembly programs in the auditorium from November through March. The custodian couldn't find or repair the problem. Even though everyone dreaded attending, there were never any cancellations or movements to other locations.

One day, approximately seven years after the onset of this debacle, parents' association members toured the boiler room with the custodian to determine if they could find the solution. Sure enough, a simple turn of a switch from off to on was all that was necessary to solve a seven-year problem.

The ancient coal-heated building often had one or more of its three boilers in disrepair. It got so cold in some rooms that classes had to be combined in warmer ones. Since it felt like twenty below, a staff member called the media to expose these horrid conditions. The very next day, after local television stations videotaped and aired the scene, the boiler was miraculously fixed. However, it did take two days for the icicles to melt.

To this day there are several rooms that receive little or no heat, especially after long weekends and holidays despite the conversion to oil heating, except in May and June when heating can be abundant.

FIGHTING MAD
AND DOWN
FOR THE COUNT

When dining out a patron may read the menu pointing out the "catch of the day."

In my school we used to see a "fight of the day" in many classes. Arguments, one-on-one fights, full-scale brawls, and melees were not uncommon. What causes these altercations?

Usually a "diss"—disrespect, a roll of the eyes, or a reference to someone's mother—is all that is needed. I wonder how many potential fights are aborted by teachers. It is extremely stressful to work in an environment knowing that a fight may break out at any time.

When I notice the first sign of possible confrontation, I send one student, generally the one closest to the door, out of the room. Since there have been so many battles over the years I'll just recount the most memorable ones.

The one that you might recall involved a wrestling match between a student and teacher, which received widespread media coverage. After the incident, the child's mother came in and allegedly shoved and threatened the teacher. The teacher then applied for an order of protection against the student, but the court denied the application. As a compromise, the student was transferred to another school immediately; the teacher exited shortly thereafter to another school in the district.

What you probably didn't know was that observers from the State Education Department were present and witnessed the incident. Furthermore, at that moment, an irate parent was arguing with a teacher, but the assistant principal intervened.

It was discovered that the regular teacher had been absent on the day in question and the child had been detained by a substitute teacher, who had no prior knowledge about the requirement of advance notification. Talk about lack of communication. The evaluaters also observed this incident. To make matters worse, two classes were brawling in the hall during the change of periods and several boys were accosted by high school students at lunch time and relieved of their jackets. These were considered the preliminary events that led up to the main event.

Another series of misadventures occurred one day in the late 1980s. The assistant principal of special and general education shared a fourth floor office. Each administrator had called for a parent at approximately the same time on unrelated matters concerning their children. What was not known was that the two parents had a long-standing feud— with each other.

Before you could say round one, the parents were grappling in the corridor outside the office. Valiant efforts were made to separate them to no avail. The security guards had to call the police. Mrs. Early, a conscientious teacher, heard the commotion and came out of her room to investigate. She noticed a jacket lying on the ground near her door and assumed it belonged to a student in her homeroom. She picked up the jacket and locked it in the clothing closet until the class returned from the gymnasium.

While the police were called on the matter mentioned above, another pair of officers was already in the building chasing two students who were accused of robbing a nearby bodega. Simultaneously, the principal received a complaint that a male teacher had sexually harassed three female students. The police eventually broke up the fight and the ladies were about to reconcile when one said, "Where's my coat?" They started to fight again!

While strolling through the corridor one morning, I heard vociferous shouting in unison. One, two, three, four.... As the numbers increased, the voices grew louder. I realized that it was coming from my homeroom class, now in mathematics. Could they have been playing some kind of game? As I got closer, I heard eight, nine, and ten! As I opened the door, I noticed that one of the students was on the floor, while the rest were scurrying to their seats.

I was informed that one student had punched another one, knocking her to the floor. They did what any good boxing crowd would do. They counted her out!

COMBAT PAY

After relating some of my experiences to members of the lay public, a common response was that you should receive combat pay. Almost every teacher, at one time or another, has broken up a fight or seen one broken up. This does not even take into account the numerous near fights that are adjudicated by the teacher. This is what makes the job so stressful contrary to public opinion.

Students bring in a multitude of problems with them. The fact that they are in school might alleviate some of the problems but does not totally eliminate them. Many students enter the school building with a great deal of hostility and anger, and it doesn't take much to set them off. A look, a roll of the eyes, or a reference to one's mother is all it takes.

Teachers are in dilemma. They are instructed by the union not to break up fights, lest they be seriously injured. On the other hand, the administration and common sense dictate that you must do something. Teachers often rely on deans, assistant principals, other teachers, security guards, and even students during crises. Nevertheless, many instructors jump right in and are frequently injured in the line of duty.

My school sometimes resembles an armed camp. We have in our employ a full-time policeman, six security guards, five assistant principals, and several aides, all armed with walkie-talkies and cell phones. This greatly reduces the problems of maintaining safety, but is by no means a panacea. At times, it seems like everyone needs their own personal security guard. At other times, everything is quite peaceful. We also possess a metal detector, which can scan students at random for weapons of class destruction. There are students who carry knives and box cutters in order to protect themselves. We've also had guns and axes brought in on occasion. As one student wrote in an essay on violence prevention, "We need more metal detectives."

During my thirty-plus years of teaching, I've been injured approximately fifteen times attempting to separate combatants. Most of the damage occurred early in my career when, as an aggressive, young teacher, I'd jump in the middle immediately. I've also witnessed and heard about other pedagogues getting injured in the line of duty in and that's just in my school.

For example, one day a student went berserk and pummeled an elderly teacher when reprimanded for poor behavior. The teacher was hospitalized for several weeks, while the student returned after a brief suspension.

Another memorable incident occurred when a class alighted from a bus after returning home from a trip. An older student began to intimidate a child three years his junior. The teacher told the student where to go. The student did, but returned within minutes brandishing a gun. He fired several shots at the teacher but fortunately missed. The teacher was transferred to another school because his safety could not be guaranteed. The perpetrator was never arrested and eventually returned to the building. What kind of message does that send?

Once a first-year teacher asked a student to remove his hat. When he refused, she removed it for him. Before you could blink, the student leaped from his chair and began to choke her mercilessly. It took several security guards and students to pull him off her and restrain him.

The most hair-raising incident of all transpired during an after-school detention program. Students who were late for school were required to serve a forty-minute detention period in the auditorium at the conclusion of the school day. The teacher on duty claimed that two girls were running on the stage. He tried to stop them by grabbing their arm and shoulder after they refused to obey his oral commands. One girl ran home crying hysterically, screaming that the teacher molested her.

Ten minutes later, her father and nine of his cohorts entered the school looking for the teacher. Each one was armed with a hand gun ready to shoot on sight, no questions asked. Fortunately for the intended victim, the principal saw what was happening and radioed the police instantaneously. The police responded within seconds and the posse scattered. However, the teacher was arrested and spent a good portion of the overnight in the station house, union representative at his side, before his release in the wee hours of the morning. He, too, was transferred to another school.

The next day the students were claiming victory and were boasting how they got rid of that teacher and any other teacher who didn't like it would be next. A pedagogue at our school informed us that a similar event occurred at her previous school. Students even invented stories to get unpopular teachers off the payroll, she alleged. As for this case, the charges against the teacher were dropped without any media attention.

There have been many other incidents: like the student who swung a meat cleaver at another outside the school's entrance; the one who entered with an ax (to grind?), looking for revenge against another student; and a pupil who punched the chief security officer and then smashed a window above the clothing closet to ensure his escape.

Once an intruder slammed a door in my face, breaking my nose. These events can lead many teachers to suffer from hypertension, colitis, nervous, and personality disorders. The stress of the job and incredibly high noise levels, particularly in the halls and cafeteria, can result in physical problems, which the Department of Education refuses to acknowledge. Perhaps a longitudinal study should be made and some type of combat pay or heart bill that other unions have should be in effect.

For the most part, the public has no clue as to what is going on. They think that school is the same as when they attended, or these are just isolated incidences. They couldn't be more wrong. Just check the number of reported incidents each year and then try to determine how many were not reported. These cover-ups do not happen at all schools, but they do occur frequently, not just in a handful of schools as the public is led to believe.

EDUCATION MAKES STRANGE BEDFELLOWS

Are you aware that politics and education have a lot in common? You probably guessed it by now. Like the typical office romance, the educational force has some really bizarre sexual encounters.

Mr. Hamilton and Mrs. Stern are a case in point. Both appeared to be happily married and each had several children. Staff members were always whispering about what was going on behind closed doors and one teacher opened that unlocked door and caught them in the act. The students were even more convinced. They referred to her as Mrs. Hamilton.

Mr. White was carrying on with Mrs. Denton for years. He seemed oblivious to the fact that everyone but his wife knew what was going on. White and Denton were often seen together, not only at work, but at diners, shopping malls, and other places of mutual consent including a nearby motel. One day as the two love birds exited their room, the principal entered an adjoining one with one of his paramours.

Mr. Ebersole, another administrator, propositioned every female substitute teacher, promising continuous employment if they succumbed. Ebersole, who was married, also carried on a long-term affair with Ms. Durant, a newly assigned first-year teacher. Yes, Mr. Ebersole was the chief "morality officer" at the school and a Sunday school teacher as well. He had apparently taken the "hypocritic oath."

These are highlights of some of the affairs that have surfaced over the years. There are countless others that people know of and pay lip to service to and others that are still the dark, dirty little secret of educators.

ONE IF BY LAND

What concerns most school officials is image. The majority of administrators care only about how things look. When it comes to how things really are, their heads are often buried deep in the sand with the rest of the ostriches. With that thought in mind, it would only be natural for them to quiver in their boots when they find out that…the evaluators are coming!

The evaluation comes from the state, city, district, and federal departments of education. Each group, checklist in hand or on a clipboard, is generally looking for something to criticize. If they didn't, their work would be useless and they would be on the unemployment line. Many evaluators don't have a clue to what's really going on in the schools. They are frequently novices to classroom situations and are often led by the administration to selected teachers. A true evaluation should be an unannounced visit by a team of veteran educators who tour a school at random. This does transpire on occasion, but most of the time, school authorities are apprised well in advance of an impending visit. Whether it's by design or the information is leaked, school officials know that the district team is coming next Wednesday or the State Education Department is visiting two weeks from Friday. What makes it even more humorous is that quite often, teachers are also aware of it and are told to be prepared, or else!

One year, the principal was expecting a district evaluation team in November. Mr. Wendell would have well positioned spies, warning him of their approach. Scouts were placed in strategic positions: on the roof, outside the main entrance, in the school yard, across the street, and perhaps at the district office to signal that "they're on their way." It's almost like warning the troops of an invasion. They're driving up the boulevard or they are using the back route. You see that limo?

What drove the principal crazy was that for whatever reason(s), the evaluators kept postponing the visit. "We'll be here next week" became next month. Mr. Wendell was on pins and needles and he made the staff feel his discomfort. This feeling filtered down to the student body until everyone was hostile for months. Perhaps the district planned this as a subterfuge to drive the principal crazy or out of the school. At any rate, weeks turned into months and no team appeared. Countless calls were made daily to the district office, trying to get a handle on the situation, to no avail.

Finally, in late June, weary from eight months of torment and worry, Wendell gave up and assumed they wouldn't be coming. How could they? The senior class had already graduated. Teachers were working on next year's records and all the student work posted on the bulletin boards, the absolute pride of the principal, was in the trash. After all, it was June 24.

On June 25, a harried principal announced to the staff, "Remove all student work from the refuse cans and rehang it immediately. The team is on its way!"

PATTERNS
OF ABSENCE

If administrators spent as much time in trying to upgrade the education of students as they do in charting such nonsensical items as employee absence patterns, perhaps student achievement and employee morale would be higher.

"Mr. Simon, did you know that you've been absent during six snowstorms? Mrs. Quincy, you have been out for three ice storms! Mr. Belinsky, did you realize that you've been out of work many Fridays and Mondays? Spending long weekends at the cottage? Were you aware that before and after every holiday you have not been here, Ms. Washington? Perhaps you should be a travel agent. Mr. Calhoun, tell me why you're only absent on Thursdays. Miss Patrick, you have been out alternate Wednesdays during even numbered months. Isn't that odd? Even Mr. Muller has been absent on rainy Tuesdays." Get the picture?

Where do they find the time or inclination to do this? What are they going to derive from intimidating and treating us like children? It was discovered with the assistance of a three-hundred-dollar-a-day consultant that Miss Jackson's pattern was that she actually had no pattern. Therefore, she must be guilty of trying to beat the system. "Being absent every weekday twice during different weather conditions renders you patternless! What are you trying to pull, Miss J?"

Instead of treating people humanely and offering constructive criticism, some administrators try to lord it over the teachers. Perhaps they're on a power trip. Maybe it's their ego, or lack of it.

At any rate, it's difficult and dangerous for suburbanites to venture out during severe weather conditions, especially when schools in their neighborhoods are closed. Many manage to get to work on such days, but I believe it's a matter of individual choice.

If I haven't already mentioned it, the warnings and threats usually arrive as a letter for your personal file. The very words that make many teachers cringe: a letter for your file! There are form letters for every possible condition: absence, lateness, snow, rain, hurricanes, tornadoes, lunch duty tardiness, letting students out without a pass, bearing in mind that it was never investigated that the students in question may have never arrived to class in the first place.

As I write, the unthinkable has occurred. The blizzard of 1996 has closed down the school system for the first time in over twenty years. What about patterns of teaching and learning?

WILL THE REAL ASSISTANT PRINCIPAL PLEASE STAND UP?

In June 1986, Mr. Glauber was in a state of euphoria. The school board had just selected him as the new assistant principal over two worthy candidates in an extremely close vote. Miss Johnson and Mr. Worthington also had aspirations for the coveted position and were naturally disappointed. Bitter feelings developed between the three because all were veteran teachers who were more than qualified for the post.

When we returned from the summer vacation, Mr. Glauber was in a state of shock. He discovered that he was not yet officially the assistant principal because the local school board had failed to vote on the matter at their last meeting in June. A mere formality, thought Mr. G.

However, due to a series of complicated circumstances, the voting never took place. Due to political infighting, the board could not get a quorum to have an official and binding vote.

Also, several board members failed to attend the September meeting. By mid October the board had been taken over (superseded) by the chancellor's office for irregularities and violations of school law.

Eventually the trustees declared the AP selection null and void and restarted the process from square one. Mr. Glauber was livid. "They'll hear from my lawyers," he screamed. Mr. Worthington was now an interim acting assistant principal at another school and Miss Johnson, still teaching at the school, seemed stoic about the messy situation.

Mr. Worthington had already been the beneficiary of a farewell party for his long and devoted service to the school. After three months of battle, Mr. W. was selected and the board of trustees immediately ratified the vote. Worthington returned to the school and, to add insult to injury, became Mr. Glauber's immediate supervisor. Miss Johnson soon transferred to another district. Glauber remained at the school, but the ill will that was created by the political process of selecting an administrator could still be felt.

You would think that education would be devoid of politics. However, allegations of payoffs for jobs and cronyism and nepotism run rampant in some districts. Political influence and who you know in some cases qualified you for being principal or assistant principal.

Sub Service

On any given day, in a large school system, teachers will be absent for a variety of reasons. In their stead, substitute teachers are hired on a per diem basis to teach a class or program for that particular day. If the regular teacher is out for a few days or an extended period of time, then a long-term sub may be hired. He then becomes the irregular teacher.

We all know that the substitute teacher has the most difficult job in the school. He/she really doesn't know the children well or at all unless this person has been a fixture in the school. Even if the teacher is familiar with the students, what hold does he/she have over them? That is why most substitutes don't work out well. It takes an exceptional teacher, one who can captivate an audience and still be stern enough to combat discipline problems, to succeed as a sub.

In many schools, the administration would prefer to have their own staff members cover classes for absentee teachers. This gives teachers on staff a chance for extra income and students know that the teacher can hold them somewhat accountable for work and behavior. On the other hand, some schools are run so chaotically that some subs refuse to work in them.

Over the years, my school had a countless number of substitute teachers. Some were good; most were awful. Let me now recount some of the more memorable teachers who offered sub or sub-par service.

Mr. Seigel had just lost his engineering job during the winter of 1974. What could he do to make ends meat? Naturally, he dusted off his substitute teaching license and was hired for the day. On this chilly February morning, he was assigned a shop program, woodworking, I believe. As he attempted to break up an altercation between two students who were flinging wood at each other, the class apparently turned on him and chased him coatless out of the building into the winter frost. Rumor has it that he's still running.

Mr. Deutsch was a strange sort of individual, which is not totally out of character for many subs. He boasted how long he'd been doing sub work and what a great teacher he was. After physically threatening students, throwing one's book bag out of a fourth floor window, and discussing items of sexual nature to fifth graders, Mr. D. was summarily dismissed. He was persona non grata at the school and district. Yet, a year later, we learned that he resurfaced at another middle school across town and was arrested for making obscene and lewd gestures.

Mr. Nielsen was an academic who was extremely weird. Most of his lessons touched on the Bermuda Triangle, black hole, or how the Rockefellers were conspiring against the citizens of New York. Many students feared him and refused to enter the room. Nielsen soon left to teach high school.

Mr. McDonnell, a musician by trade, often subbed between gigs. His remarkable resemblance to a children's toy earned him the nickname Mr. Potato Head. Mr. PH was the butt of some cruel jokes, but miraculously survived for several years.

The quickest exit belongs to Mr. Weinstock. Mr. W., a recent college graduate, was assigned an English program for the day. After experiencing a ten-minute homeroom class, he disappeared without a word and was never seen again.

One of the most bizarre subs was an elderly woman who was based at the Port Authority bus terminal. Anytime she had to be reached, she was called at a public telephone booth near the terminal lockers. Perhaps she was homeless or had emotional problems. Nevertheless, she was employed for many years as a sub.

It's difficult to remember the names of all the substitutes who ever taught at my school since they are rarely formally introduced to the staff. One sub continued his lesson while a fire raged through the room. Another crawled under a bathroom stall to introduce herself to a colleague. One had a wig removed and tossed on to a tree in the side yard. Another was terminated for kicking a student in the rear when challenged to do so. Once, a paraprofessional was hired as a sub even though she was still employed as a para in another school. Finally, a man named Mr. Black, who was white, filled in for Mr. White, who was black.

It's simple to see how sub service got its name. However, if you're gifted, creative, and experienced, the job may be just for you, if you have the proper credentials.

SILENT READING

When I attended school, it was assumed that when you read something to yourself, the reading would be silent. Not so with today's breed of students. Silence is a rare commodity, especially during reading class, which most students dislike. The primary reasons for this abhorrence are that many pupils find reading boring or they don't read very well. It's dull and a waste of their precious time. They would rather play video games, log on to a computer's WWF website, hang out, or just socialize.

Research documents that the more time one spends on a particular task, the greater the ability becomes. Therefore, many schools have instituted a quiet or silent reading program. Reading is stressed because of low standardized test scores, which causes a great deal of distress to principals. The silence is emphasized to enable students, many with limited attention spans, to read in a pleasant, quiet atmosphere, to which many are unaccustomed. Sounds plausible, right? Like many programs, it usually sounds better on paper than its implementation.

Having observed and experienced "silent reading programs" under the realm of several principals, I have noticed the following: When asked to bring interesting, wholesome reading material to school, the majority of children either forgot or did not care to bring anything at all. As a result, the teacher had to supply them with books and magazines.

During a selected period, everyone, including the teacher, would cease whatever they were doing and read silently for pleasure. The teacher modeled the reading, which was supposed to last forty-five minutes. I must confess that in some cases, it lasted a mere forty-five seconds, if that. Many students were not silent and a large percentage were not reading, even though they brought or received the necessary material. This debacle occurred after motivational discussions by administrators, teachers, and guidance personnel about the importance of the silent reading program.

A good idea failed and the period eventually turned into the usual mandated assigned work from the teacher. However, I have been advised that the program works well in other schools, where the learning climate was superior.

Perhaps reverse psychology should have been used. Just tell the students that talking was permitted and no reading shall be done. Since many adolescents do the opposite of what is required, it might work.

Seriously, silent reading is an excellent concept and should be implemented successfully in the elementary and middle schools.

To SURR
with Love?

No, it's not the movie. It's the real thing. The acronym SURR stands for School Under Registration Review, which means nightmares for principals and staffs. If a school is even mentioned for SURR candidacy, then all hell breaks loose. This simply means that for a variety of reasons, the school is "failing" state standards. Thus, the state has the power to take the school over, or at the very least, reorganize the building.

Most principals fear being on the list because it means that big brother will be observing every move and their autonomy and power will be diminished. Furthermore, many view it as a reflection upon themselves and their polices. Yet it is not uncommon for many schools to be on this dreaded list. At any given time, perhaps fifteen to twenty percent of all schools are on the list or headed in that direction.

Generally, a school is on the hit list for a combination of offenses such as: low or declining standardized test scores, poor attendance, high drop-out rates, teacher dissatisfaction, and a large number of incident reports that feature assaults, injuries, assorted crimes and arrests for weapons possession. Once a school is on the list, it is quite difficult to escape. The school has to dramatically improve in all areas of concern within a specified time period (three to five years) or be reorganized into a different type of learning environment such as sub schools, academies, mini schools, or magnet schools. The principal has no choice but to comply with state regulations. He/she must organize committees of staff, parent, and student participants to form a comprehensive, viable plan that will quickly turn the school around. The plan must be submitted and approved by the State Education Department.

Meanwhile, the state sends in its hired guns to survey the school on a regular basis in order to monitor progress and shore up weaknesses. These constant visits make everyone feel uptight. One time a state monitor witnessed three major brawls on one floor within fifteen minutes. Eventually, the monitor entered an adjoining classroom for his own safety.

Another time, when a group of ten was touring the building on their initial visit, a small fire broke out in a cafeteria trash bin. The fire was allegedly started by a student in the school. Although the fire was quelled immediately, the odor of smoke filtered upstairs, right under the noses of the State Education Department members. The principal calmly assured everyone over the public address system that a small fire, which started in a dumpster outside the building, was now under control. That was a close call. I could just see the headlines in the paper the next day. FIRE IN OUT-OF-CONTROL SCHOOL—STATE ED. MEMBERS FLEE FOR LIVES!

Once a school gets labeled SURR, it's quite difficult to rid itself of that reputation. Everything is under a microscope and you get constant evaluations from the state, city, and district. At its worst, the school will lose its accreditation. This means total reorganization; new administrators, staff, and concepts for learning. The worst scenario is that the school may actually close. In this type of reorganization, some staff members may be retained, but most will be asked to look for employment elsewhere, and if the principal remains or stays in the system, he/she will be subject to retraining. In some cases the number of the school changes along with all or most of the administrators as well as fifty percent of the staff.

As a result, it's no wonder that to SURR with love has a special meaning for educators.

DECENTRALIZATION

In 1969 decentralization sounded like a great idea; local community school boards would control the day-to-day running of the elementary and intermediate schools in their district. Wouldn't that be better than all the bureaucratic red tape encountered at the central board? Wouldn't it be more effective to manage schools from the neighborhood than from downtown?

Another favorable aspect would be to defuse racial confrontations caused by the 1968 teacher strike. The political powers that be believed that this type of program would counteract the hostilities that developed in many communities.

More than thirty years have passed since the onset of decentralization. What was once considered a panacea for an ailing school is presently being eliminated by the Department of Education. One mayor desired to "blow up" the entire system and the next one wrested control of the system from the community school boards.

Over the years there had been countless scandals involving local school board policies and actions. Allegations of theft, no-show jobs, misappropriation of funds, nepotism, and intimidation to purchase tickets for fund-raising events were among the most serious charges. The phrases of "it's who you know and not what you know" ran rampant, especially in selecting school administrators. Current politicians from mayor on down wanted the process reformed, particularly the local school board election procedures. With the mayoral control now in effect, it appears that the advocates for reform have triumphed.

On the surface community control sounded like a fantastic idea. Local school boards were to control, operate, and monitor the education of the children in their own communities. This was supposed to improve all areas of the educational process. The results have been for the most part, in my opinion, disastrous. Scandal plagued districts in many areas have seemed to place their personal interest ahead of the children they were supposed to serve. I'm certain that there were many well-meaning and dedicated members, but from what we read and heard from the media, the abuse of power seemed widespread.

Perhaps local board members viewed decentralization as a way to wrest power from the central board and get a piece of the pie for themselves. Political infighting, often drawn along racial and ethnic lines, occurred frequently. This caused deals to be made while the best educational decisions were sometimes overlooked. Some school board members considered schools in their districts as their personal fiefdoms.

Are the test scores, attendance records, and behavioral tendencies better than they were prior to decentralization? I think not. Many schools have been taken over by the state and have been mandated to reorganize their entire system of educating students and training teachers. Buildings are in decay and some are literally falling apart. The chancellors have superseded local boards at various times for a myriad of infractions.

Educators were initially excited about the prospect of decentralization in the late 1960s but many pundits correctly predicted widespread corruption because they believed it was essentially an appeasement policy for certain segments of the community.

Decentralization was not a total failure. It did work in some areas of the city that were not often publicized. However, to succeed on a citywide basis, reforms had to be made that previous administrations could not effect.

It now appears that the thirty-year-plus run of community control is about to come to an end, barring any unforeseen last-minute developments or lawsuit directives.

DOWN BY THE OLD MAIN STREAM

I n the late 1990s everything was in the downsizing mode, including education. Besides having budgets cut to the bone at the city, state, and federal levels, there was an outcry to decrease the total number of students in special education as well as increasing class size for that population.

According to the politicians, the aforementioned would serve dual purposes. First, federal spending would be drastically reduced. Whether you realize it or not, the average special education student receives three to four times the funding as the one in general education. Secondly, the argument that the special education student is "trapped" and will never leave the program has some merit, though it's not always the case.

Special education students are supposed to be evaluated every two or three years by a special committee on the handicapped. If they are deemed ready, they are eligible to join the general education population in part or totally. This process is called mainstreaming. However, even before the evaluation occurs, many special education children are mainstreamed into the least restrictive environment whenever possible.

I should know because since 1975, I've had many mainstreamed students in my class.

More often than not, they try hard and are generally better behaved than the average general education students. However, a pet peeve of mine was that very little information was exchanged between the mainstreamed teacher and special education personnel despite assurances to the contrary. I was usually told that she's wonderful, but little else about the background of the student. I was never privy to the IEP (Individual Education Program), which all special education students and teachers have. Furthermore, I was not told what problems, if any, I might have to encounter or how to handle them. Also, there were infrequent meetings or follow-up sessions conducted by the Special Education Division to see how their kids were doing.

It seemed to me that mainstreaming was a "dumping ground" and a convenient way for the special education department to fulfill its legal obligation of placing challenged students in their least restrictive environment.

The concept of mainstreaming is an excellent one. It's just that more feedback must occur between all the parties involved. Perhaps it does in other schools. There should be mandatory biweekly conferences between teachers, administrators, evaluators, guidance personnel, school-based support team members and other interested members of the committee on the handicapped. These conferences should be beneficial to the students and teachers and could even be held by the "old main stream."

An Open-
and-Shut Case

On a typical wintry morning with precipitation falling mercilessly, I'd look out my window and witness a frozen wasteland. Driving conditions are treacherous and the mayor advises people to remain at home, but city schools are open. Why? All the nearby suburban districts are closed or at least have delayed openings. What makes this school system so different? Isn't it just as dangerous for students and staff to travel as it is for those in other systems?

One can only speculate about political, financial, or practical reasons, but the general mindset is that if you're alive, you are supposed to report for work regardless of the conditions or threat of personal safety. If not, you may receive a letter for your file or a reprimand if a pattern of absence on snow days develops. Not that it matters, but if you are in an accident and injured, you might be out for weeks or months. That possibility is unimportant. The only thing that matters is that you arrive any way you can during a snow or ice storm.

While most other school systems are rational and care about the personal safety of its staff and students, it's curious that the large city does not. They may offer a multitude of reasons for this. The city is different. You can take public transportation; you should live nearby; why are you afraid of snow and ice? Perhaps part of this is true. I wonder. Could it be that it's inconvenient for city parents to arrange for day care? What about parents in other communities? Don't they have similar problems? Maybe it has something to do with the breakfast and lunch programs, which are federally funded. Could it be that the system wants the employees to use a sick day so as to reduce the amount in his/her bank, which would be profitable for the city?

So, what happens when you miraculously arrive on stormy days? Generally, one half to two thirds of the students smartly remain at home. Your reward for risking your life is an extra teaching period or two for absentee teachers or teaching combined classes of mixed registers. Other smaller rewards are cleaning off your car, driving in hazardous conditions, and "babysitting" a few kids or mixed classes that you've never seen before. God forbid you arrive late! People have been docked pay for tardiness when they should be worshipped for just getting there alive. It's standard operating procedure for the system and its principals to intimidate teachers in this manner. There's nothing in the contract about loss of pay or reprimands if such a pattern develops.

Furthermore, several snow days are built into the yearly calendar and are almost never used. Most city teachers work one hundred and eighty six or more days, while their suburban counterparts work five or six fewer under superior conditions and greater remuneration. The point is, why not cancel school and make up the days, if necessary, at a more prudent time?

Schools are open for one hundred and eighty-plus days when weather conditions are favorable. Are the students learning and retaining what they've been taught at such an advanced level? Then why risk lives and safety during dangerous storms?

We always pondered what would occur during a catastrophic event? Would schools be open? Finally, during the blizzard of 1996 schools were allotted two snow days and a delayed opening after nearly twenty years of abstinence.

THE HENCHMEN

Most city schools employ teachers who are out of the classroom working in various administrative or quasi-administrative positions. They may be mentors, staff developers, testing coordinators, programmers, drop-out prevention counselors for at-risk students, or administrative assistants to the principal. Over the years the administrative assistants, through no fault of their own, rarely or ever teach classes and become ensconced in a powerful position. In short, many of them become the principal's henchman.

The henchman or lady often does the dirty work and dastardly deeds that the principal does not want to be held accountable for, lest employee morale decline even further. The henchman metes out the rotten assignments and informs you of your daily tasks and extra workload (clerical or teaching), usually in a cold, Nazi-like manner. There are some henchmen who are pleasant, smile to your face, but achieve the same results. They've created their own power structure within the principal's fiefdom, performing necessary tasks, but nevertheless, becoming full of themselves.

The longer the henchman becomes entrenched, the more powerful he becomes. He has the principal's ear on every matter and often recommends tasks, schedules, and positions for other staffers. Sometimes you begin to wonder who the real principal is. Also, don't cross him or you may wind up with the worst program next year and become persona non grata in the clique of inner circle employees.

Many pedagogues fear the henchman, even though he's just a teacher. They are not administrators but wield as much, if not more, power. Don't misunderstand. Most henchmen are extremely qualified but should be teaching a minimum of one to two classes per day.

When one sits in an ivory tower, it's always easy to criticize and belittle those who are on the front lines. It's simple for a henchman to forget what it was like to teach a regular full-time program. They often say that when they were teaching fifteen years ago that they never had these problems. Maybe that's true to a certain extent.

Times and students have changed dramatically over the past ten to fifteen years. Today's students are much more difficult than those of even five years ago. They come in with a multitude of problems, both personal and familial. So, for the henchmen to mock and denigrate teacher performances on a regular basis, one would think that is truly an injustice.

IV

THE FINAL CHAPTER

ERASING THE BLACKBOARD

If I had a dollar for every time I asked a student to erase the blackboard, I'd be a rich man. So would countless other teachers. It's a simple request and task; or is it?

Mrs. Allison, a traveling teacher, happened to conduct a lesson in Miss Rogers' room. As the lesson ended, Allison had to rush to her next class, and in doing so, made a fatal mistake. She neglected to do something extremely important, according to Miss Rogers. Miss Rogers discovered to her horror that Allison had failed to erase the blackboard. Rogers was frantic. She or one of her students would have to erase the work from the previous class. How insulting! She told Allison just that, after she left her class unattended to hunt her down.

Allison could not believe that Rogers was making her oversight into such an issue. The two had words and Rogers left in a huff. She stormed into her supervisor's office complaining vociferously, demanding punishment and reparations immediately. The shocked supervisor attempted to calm Rogers down, but failed. Dissatisfied, Rogers scampered to the union representative to file a grievance. The union leader stared at her incredulously and asked, "Are you serious?" Undaunted, Rogers answered in the affirmative.

World War III had just commenced due to the oversight or lack of time in erasing a blackboard. With the world and the school systems having so many problems, it would seem that this atrocity should rank right up there in importance.

I wonder if the blackboard ever got erased or if Rogers' students received any instruction that period. Perhaps I'll look in the room and comment, "Nice blackboard." Or, maybe we should send Miss Rogers a lifetime supply of board erasers.

What are we coming to? We now have two teachers embroiled in a bitter dispute over something so simple that a preschool child could handle. Possibly, the problem is much deeper and the lack of erasure symbolized the "other" problem.

Nevertheless, this incident shows a complete lack of maturity, professionalism, and sanity on the part of Rogers. Furthermore, when children view this model of behavior, it's no wonder their attitudes become further distorted.

And so it goes. Just another chapter in the blackboard bungle.

Printed in the United States
29303LVS00001B/190